©2018 Julia Geens

Sadie The Spider

ISBN: 978-1-9999872-0-6

sadiethespider.com

Illustration and design by Sarah-Leigh Wills.
happydesigner.co.uk

Sadie The Spider

Written by
Julia Geens

Illustrated by
Sarah-Leigh Wills

Sadie the spider loves to explore,

spinning her web high up from the floor.

She found a great spot on
a window frame,

to catch a fly that
was her aim.

A man came along to do the cleaning,
washing the glass until it was gleaming.

He spotted the spider and let out a yell!
Off from the window and down Sadie fell.

"I'm scared, I'm scared" Sadie cried
and off she ran to find a place to hide.

Sadie ran to the back door of the house.
She tucked herself away as quiet as a mouse.

The lady of the house came walking through,

stopping by the door to tie up her shoe.

She spotted the spider and started to shriek

and woke poor Sadie up from her sleep.

"I'm scared, I'm scared" Sadie cried and off
she ran to find a place to hide.

Out through the door Sadie sped and hid
deep inside a flower bed.

The little boy was outside playing with his ball,

bouncing it high and watching it fall.

He spotted the spider
and let out a cry,

poor little Sadie didn't know why.

"I'm scared, I'm scared"
Sadie cried

and off she ran to find a place to hide.

Down through the garden and over the wall,

Sadie was shaking, she felt so small.

There she was hidden beneath some sticks,
when a dog came along practising his tricks.

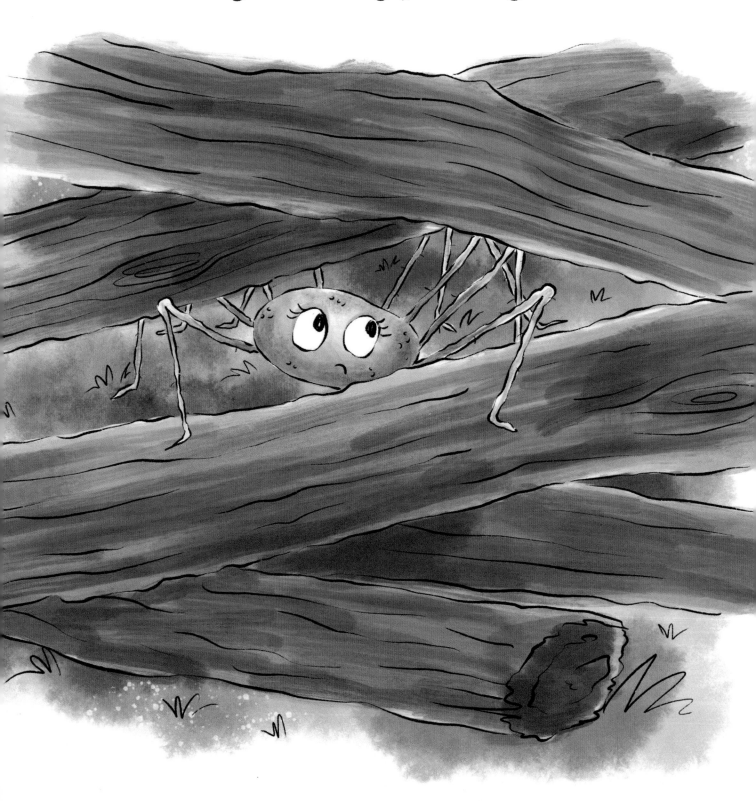

He spotted the spider and started to bark,
and up leapt Sadie straight out of the park!

"I'm scared, I'm scared" Sadie cried and
off she ran to find a place to hide.

She ran to the car at the side of the street,
as fast as she could with her tiny feet.

The little girl was out playing on the drive,
practising her kicks and dancing a jive.

She spotted the spider and started to squeal and out jumped Sadie from under the wheel.

"I'm scared, I'm scared" Sadie cried and off she ran to find a place to hide.

Down a cobbled path Sadie fled, to a rundown door which was painted red.

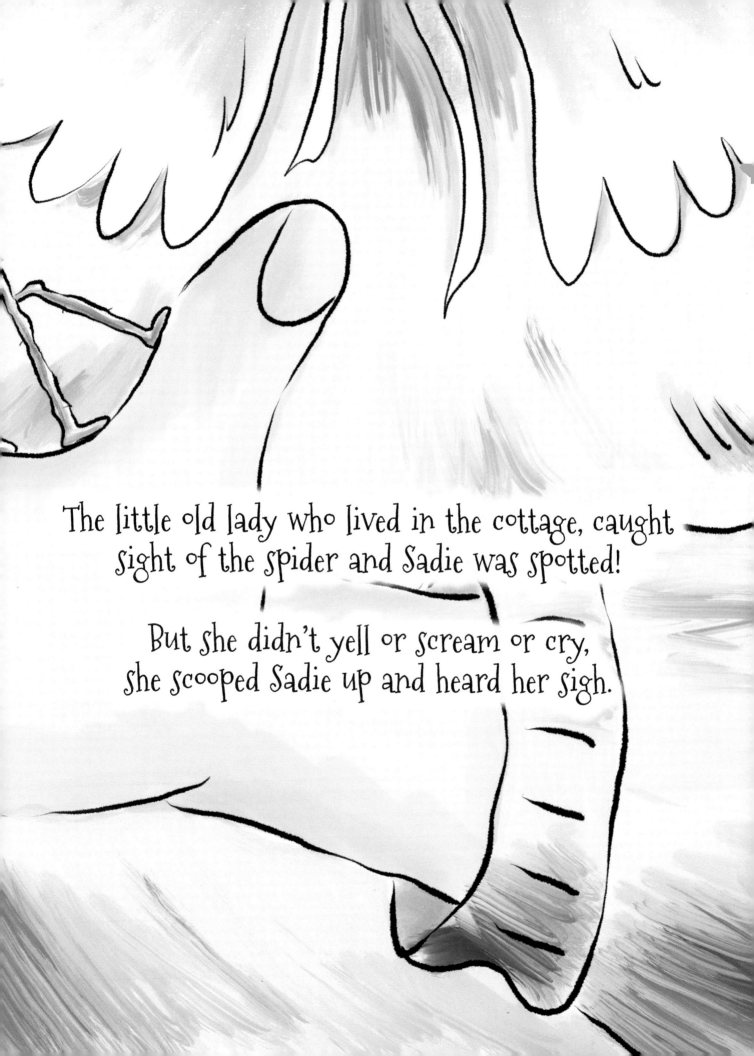

The little old lady who lived in the cottage, caught
sight of the spider and Sadie was spotted!

But she didn't yell or scream or cry,
she scooped Sadie up and heard her sigh.

"I'll try not to disturb you while you explore,
so you can spin your web high up
from the floor."

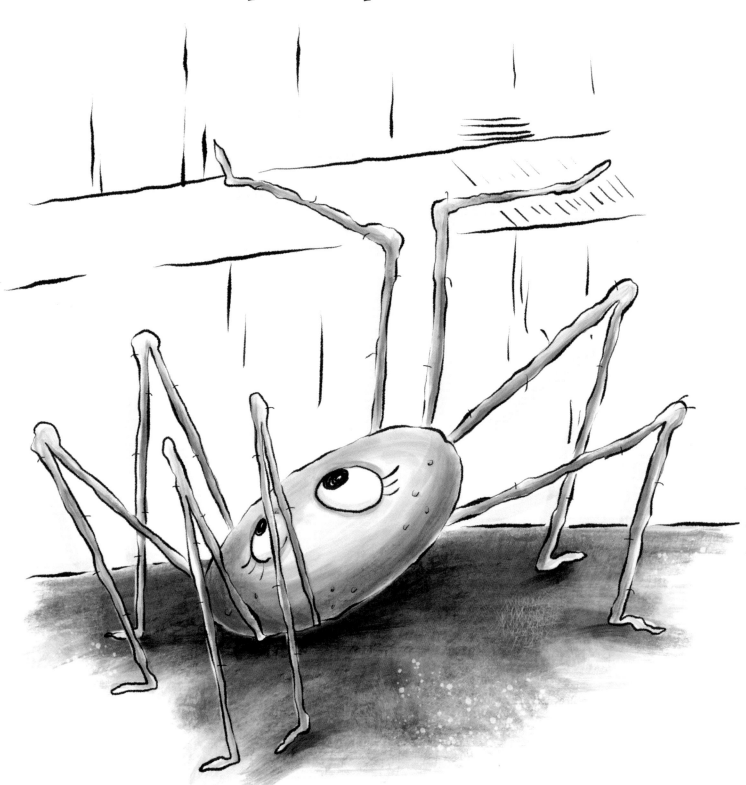

Sadie was safe and no longer scared,
She lived with a lady who really cared.

She found a great spot on a window frame,
to catch a fly that was her aim.

29161935R00020

Printed in Great Britain
by Amazon